TWO BOYS, A DOG, & A MURDER

A SHORT, SWEET MYSTERY

MALATHI MOHAN

Clever Fox®
PUBLISHING

Chennai • Bangalore

CLEVER FOX PUBLISHING
Chennai, India

Published by CLEVER FOX PUBLISHING 2025

ISBN: 978-93-7500-420-2

Cover Design and Illustrations - By Nihaarika Lunia

Dedicated to
Shri John Edathattil

He made me realize that where fiction was concerned, I should trust myself more, not less.

CONTENTS

1. Summer Hols 1
2. The Mystery Begins 5
3. The Possible Witness 10
4. The Next Step 14
5. The Children's Home 18
6. Christopher 20
7. The Letters 25
8. The Chase 30
9. Jacob 33
10. The Return 39
11. The Evidence 42
12. The Lockers 44
13. The New Tuition Master 48

Epilogue 53
Glossary 54
Why Did I Venture Into Writing This Book? 56
Acknowledgements 58
A Summary by John Edathattil 60
Reviews 63

CHAPTER 1

SUMMER HOLS

"Kausalya supraja Rama poorva sandhya pravarthathe ...."

The mellifluous voice of M.S., India's most loved singer's morning prayer was floating from a middle-class apartment in a congenial neighbourhood of Chennai. In many South Indian homes, this prayer to Lord Venkateswara is chanted in the morning.

Raj, a young boy in his early teens, was slowly waking up. His first sleepy thought was about his summer vacation and importantly, a change of the maths tuition master. He thought, "Oh God, who is it going to be next?" The last tuition master, the third one this year, had been

very strict and very boring. The previous two masters were not comfortable with Danny, who was a pup and constantly played his mischief during the tutoring, disturbing and distracting the tuition class. The boys were no less mischief makers, either! Thankfully, the masters left on their own as they got jobs abroad. Maths tuition is in high demand among most schoolchildren, as it is a difficult subject.

Praying for a better person, Raj jumped out of his bed to get ready quickly for his holiday act with his closest friend and classmate, Shri, who lived in the adjoining apartment. Raj gulped down the glass of cocoa his mother gave him, grabbed his new football, and ran out, saying he would be back for breakfast. Shri joined him, and so did Danny, their pet, and they took off before anyone could stop them.

Skipping, jumping, and running went the two boys and their excited, frisky dog. Hardly one year old, he was attached to his little master Rajesh and to his close friend Shri. A constant companion and an accomplice in all their adventures was Danny, the happiest of the three.

The boys were exuberant, excited, and full of anticipation after a fast game of football in the neighbouring field. They were now running home chasing each other. The ball slipped from Rajesh's hand and rolled towards the shackled gate of a vacant compound. All three headed towards the gate, but the boys came to a sudden halt when they saw Danny sniffing at the gate and taking a stiff stance. The wagging stopped, and he looked questioningly at the boys.

What had he seen?

CHAPTER 2

THE MYSTERY BEGINS

Raj and Shri went close to the gate and saw what looked like a leg, shoeless and motionless. It peeped out of a gunny bag. The boys were scared and decided to run away, but Danny remained stubbornly looking from the leg to the boys, as if to say, "There is something fishy here. Aren't you going to do something about it?" Raj looked around and decided to climb the gate, though Shri kept urging him not to. Right near the gate, Raj saw something shining, picked it up, and slipped it into his pocket. He told Shri to run home and fetch his father, as he would know what to do.

Shri ran fast and returned soon with Raj's father, Sumesh, and his own father, Venkat. They took one look at the scene and called the police. Sumesh instructed the boys to go home, but they pleaded to stay till the police arrived, as they were the first witnesses and were curious to know the outcome of the investigation.

The street on which the locked property stood was not a crowded one, as it was within a middle-class locality, without any shops, except for a small teashop close by. Just three men were having tea and chatting. A short distance from the gate sat a beggar on a tattered old carpet. He seemed to be minding his own business – or was he?

The police van drove up, and Sub Inspector Mani jumped out along with a couple of constables. Raj's father, Sumesh, greeted the SI and took him to the locked compound. SI Mani told the constables to climb over the gate and look around. They poked here and there and pushed open the gunny bag which revealed a body. The corpse seemed to be of a youngish man with his face covered with blood and a big wound on the head. His clothing indicated that he was from an upper-middle-class background. Nothing else could be gathered from the site. In the meantime, an ambulance arrived, as the police must have called for it. A tentative estimation of the death was made, that it might have been around 3 a.m., as the body was just showing signs of Rigor Mortis. The forensic technician looked for clues in the area, and as there were no blood spills, they felt that the murder must have been committed elsewhere. The body was loaded in the ambulance, which sped away to the forensic lab.

SI Mani turned towards the boys and the parents to collect their version of the discovery. Raj spoke up and narrated how they came running and throwing the ball to each other with Danny jumping and barking between them, and how, suddenly, Danny had led them to the body. How they were scared but decided to inform their parents first, and Shri had gone to fetch them while Raj stayed with Danny. And how with one look at the scene, Sumesh had called the police and ordered the boys to go home, but they had begged to stay as he and Shri were the first witnesses. Raj was interrupted off and on, with Shri adding his part of the escapade.

CHAPTER 3

THE POSSIBLE WITNESS

SI Mani praised the boys for their composure and sensible handling by calling their parents. He gave a pat to Danny also, as if to appreciate his part in this event. Danny proudly continued his role by sniffing around. He went towards the beggar on the opposite side and stopped suddenly, barking at him. The boys were surprised as he never barked at people. SI Mani walked towards the beggar and asked him if he had seen anything untoward. The beggar, Govind said nervously, that he only saw the boys and the dog, and later their parents. "I

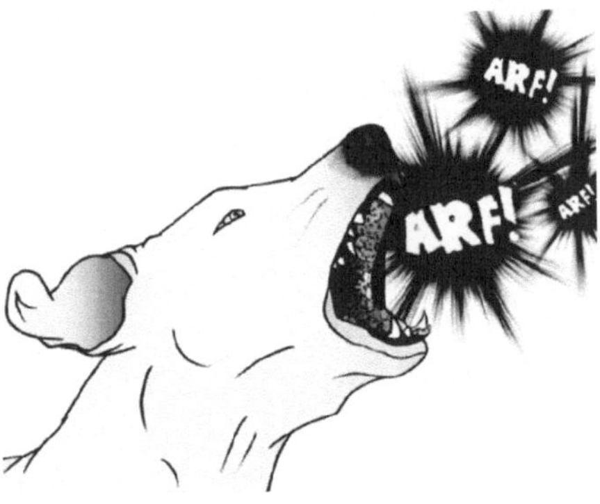

don't know anything more, Sir", he concluded. His nervousness seemed out of place to Mani. He stood there staring at the things around Govind with interest.

Suddenly, a cell phone rang, and it seemed to come from Govind's worn bag. The beggar jumped, and Danny started a low growl. Mani strode forward to ask Govind, "You have a cell phone?" "........ Yes, Sir.... No, Sir ...," Govind was stammering. "Where did you get it from?" asked Mani in a strict tone. "I picked it up from that closed gate, Sir." He was shivering and visibly nervous, glancing towards the tea shop at the end of the road.

Mani took the phone to answer with a short grunt. The caller immediately shouted, "Hey, where are you? Why haven't you called? We have been waiting since this morning." Mani answered, whispering so that his voice could not be recognised by the caller, "Can't talk

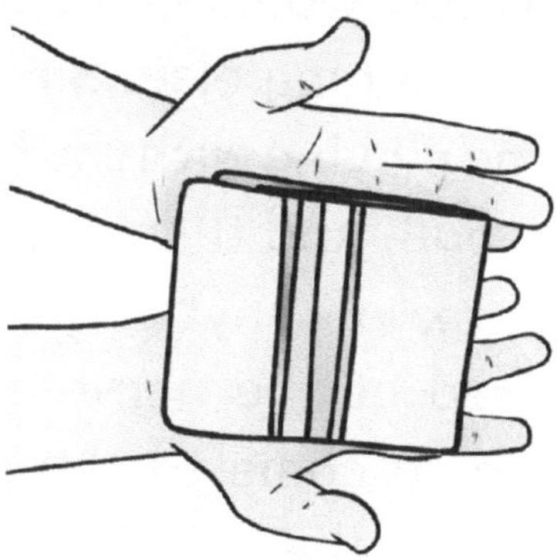

now, where shall we meet?" He listened for a few seconds, nodded his head, and then the call ended. He now had a meeting place and time, but no other details. He called his station and gave the phone number for its owner to be traced.

Mani looked at Govind, rapped him lightly on his shoulder with his baton, and asked," When did you come here and what did you see? Did you pick up anything else?" Govind was shivering," Sir, I came when the radio in the tea shop was playing some music, and the morning news was just starting. I spread out my cloth to sit when I saw the phone shining near the gate. As I picked it up, there was a wallet also, which I took, but I did not open it, Sir. That's all, Sir, and I waited to see if anybody would come searching, Sir. I did not see anything else, Sir. Yes, Sir, then the boys came playing with the ball. The dog was chasing the ball, and then everything happened. Sir, I don't know anything else. Sir, please Sir" Mani stared at the nervous beggar, "OK, OK, you need to come to the station for questioning. Get into the jeep."

"Please, Sir, I did not do anything. Sir, please let me go, Sir." "Don't worry, I'll let you off soon." "Sir, I haven't eaten anything. Sir, can I just run to the tea shop and get a bun and tea, Sir?" He looked furtively towards the shop. Perhaps, Govind had been placed there by the men in the shop to watch and to report on any developments near the closed gate? Otherwise, why would he be glancing at the shop frequently, thought Mani. "Oh, OK, Constable, get him breakfast at the station". Mani was a kind police officer, not a rude one.

Before they left, since he was doubtful about the men in the tea shop, Mani went over to talk to them. They answered his questions and told him that they often visited the shop as this was their regular meeting place and that they knew the shopkeeper. Mani looked at the shopkeeper questioningly, and he nodded in agreement.

CHAPTER 4

THE NEXT STEP

Mani opened the wallet that the beggar had handed over and pulled out a visiting card and a stub of an air ticket from Singapore to Chennai. The name on the card and the name on the ticket was Christopher. To Mani, this indicated the probable name of the person and of the company where he was employed.

Raj and Shri had been watching, and the conversation indicated to them that the corpse had a name and that he was no longer just a body, but that he was a person with an identity. Raj was nervous about the thing he had picked up earlier. He wanted to tell his father, but he did not want Mani to hear in case he got punished. Shri was also watching Raj with the same doubt and fear. Why was Raj hiding it? Both boys were always honest, so this silence was troubling them both.

SI Mani told the fathers to bring the boys to the police station nearby and took his leave. Sumesh called out to the boys and said, “Let’s go home, and after breakfast, we’ll leave for the station”. Venkat assured him that he would stay with the children and keep Sumesh informed about the developments. Everybody went back with Danny following.

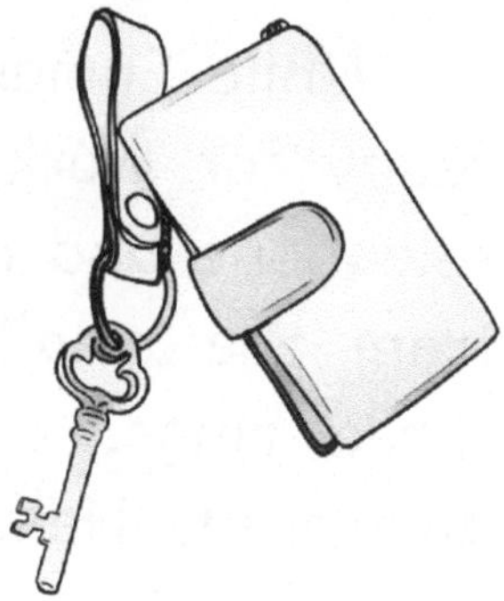

At home, after a breakfast of upma, the boys got together again on the balcony. They were eager to see what Raj had pocketed. It was a key chain with a single key and a small booklet attached to it. The book had some names and numbers which Raj noted down quickly. He put it back in his pocket. He then informed his father about it, telling him how he had picked it up from right below the gate. Sumesh asked him strictly why he had not mentioned it earlier. Raj was nervous and said, “I was scared, Appa, especially when the inspector rapped the beggar and was rudely questioning him. I wanted to tell you first." "Anything else?" demanded Sumesh. "No, Appa"said Raj, but was looking disturbed. Sumesh said in a kinder tone, "I don't want you boys to get into trouble, son; this is notchild's play. It looks like murder, and I'm unhappy that both of you are involved in finding the body, but I'm proud that you handled the problem sensibly."

While Sumesh went in for a bath to get ready for work, Raj picked up his landline telephone and rang a number he had noted from the small book. After three rings, a lady's voice answered, "Hello, St. Antony's Children's Home."

Raj was still nervous. After a pause, he asked, "May I know who is speaking?" The voice answered, "I'm Sister Mary. Who's this?" "My name is Raj, Sister. Please may I come and see you now? It's urgent." There was a long pause. Sister Mary was used to urgent and disturbed requests as this was an orphanage, and she had heard many such requests. She said, “If this is a matter related to our orphanage, you may come now. If you need the address, I’ll give it to you.” Raj took down the address and told her that, as it was close to his place, he would arrive soon with his friend, Shri, and his pet, Danny. Sr. Mary said that was fine.

Raj shouted out to his mother that he would be back by the time his dad completed his bath and Puja, saying that, he ran out with Shri and Danny.

CHAPTER 5

THE CHILDREN'S HOME

At the children's home, the watchman, Tony, had been informed to let Raj, his friend, and the dog in, so he made no fuss like security men normally do. He provided a smooth entrance while directing them to the visitors' room.

Raj greeted Sr. Mary and introduced himself, Shri, and Danny to her. She was amused to see the serious faces of these young men. Generally, her visitors were adults who came to admit young children or couples who came to adopt. However, she received them cordially, allowing Danny to find a comfortable place under the sofa at the boys' feet.

Raj looked at Sr. Mary's kind face and hesitantly started telling her about their morning's adventure regarding finding a body in the closed compound. He showed her the keychain with the little booklet, which he had found, with the following words in the first two pages. "MUST HELP, MUST RETURN" - Christopher

CHAPTER 6

CHRISTOPHER

Sr. Mary looked at the little diary on the keychain given to her by Raj. She was silent for about one minute which, seemed like an eternity to the boys. They had very little time before they had to rush back home to get ready for that dratted tuition master. Both were not too bad at math, but like all present-day parents, their parents also wanted them to get good marks in their 10th standard exam. This would help them to opt for their specialization courses.

Sr. Mary spoke at last. "Yes, this is Christopher's keychain. I had personally selected small gifts for the boys for Christmas, and this one, I chose specially for the boys who were leaving the orphanage two years ago. Christopher liked red so I gave him this one."

There was a hint of a tear in her eyes, which she ignored. “Christopher came to us when he was perhaps three years old. He had been left at our gate one morning, about 15 years back. I had gone to the gate to give a cup of tea to Tony, our night watchman, who was still snoring in his chair, and I saw this little sleeping boy, curled up near a bush. With Tony’s habit of sleepy alertness, we had no idea how the little boy had come here. When I woke both up, they were startled, and the boy didn’t even cry. He just curled up into a ball, as though he had to protect himself. He was full of scratches and wounds. His clothes were dirty, and he was afraid, very frightened, of anyone touching him.”

“With Tony’s help, I took him in, and it took a long time before he accepted a small cup of warm milk. Sr. Veronica then took charge, and it was months before he came to trust her. He was silent and scared all the time.

The local police were informed, but no one came to claim the child. He was an enigma to us for a long time. His background was never revealed, though we made many sincere attempts.

Gradually, he settled down but never made any close friends. Sr. Veronica was his closest acquaintance, and he did whatever she guided him to do. He was very helpful to all the children, but never bonded with anyone.

We tried to put him up for adoption, but Christopher used to shiver and shake when any new adults came near him. He would hold on to Sr. Veronica and refuse to let go. He never cried, but we knew there was deep sorrow inside him.

By the time he was in his early teens, he had accepted the home as his own and was ready to take up any responsibility given to him, and he also volunteered a lot more. He was the most dependable in the boys' section. He was not very good at his studies, but he always tried very hard to do better. He was able to pass his 12th standard and complete his school education.

When he reached 18, we had to send him out as per our rules. We placed him in one of our ancillary manufacturing companies, and he had to share a small apartment provided for the workers. From his small salary, Christopher used to give 25 percent to us. He used to visit us regularly for six months, and then, he disappeared for quite some time. We learned that he was no longer working at that company. Sr. Veronica was very upset, especially since she wanted to see him one last time. A couple of months later, she passed away, but she always thought of him.

We did not hear from Christopher till his letter arrived two days ago, addressed to Sr. Veronica. I kept it unopened to give back to him when he came to visit. Now you tell me that this key chain was found near the body of a young man, I hope and pray that it was not him.

I'm sure the police will come here soon. Please tell them I'll give all the cooperation they require."

Raj and Shri were now sure that the body was that of Christopher. They now understood that he had been a gentle, well-behaved person. So, how was he murdered and why? The determination to fulfil Christopher's loving gesture to Sr. Veronica became their mission.

CHAPTER 7

THE LETTERS

Shri picked himself out of his introspection after listening to Sr. Mary. He asked, “So, there’s nothing of his left here and no one else who knew him?” “No, I’m sorry... But wait, Sr. Veronica gave me a small packet to give to Christopher, if he came here”, saying which Sr. Mary went to a cupboard and took out a plastic bag. There was a diary in it; it was Christopher’s. There was also a letter from Sr. Veronica. Sr. Mary read it out to the boys.

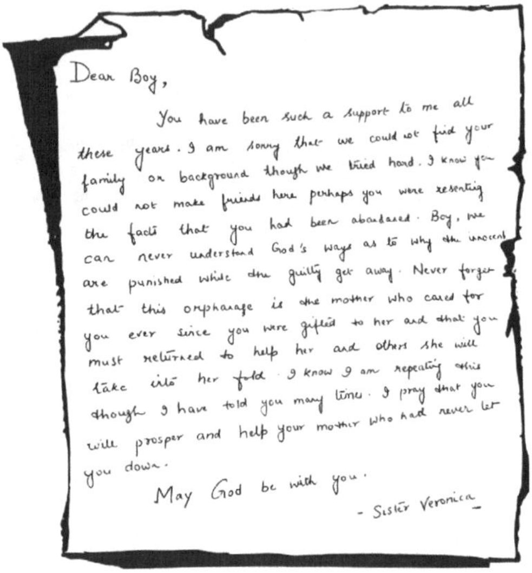

Dear Boy,

You have been such a support to me all these years. I am sorry that we could not find your family or background though we tried hard. I know you could not make friends here perhaps you were resenting the facts that you had been abandoned. Boy, we can never understand God's ways as to why the innocent are punished while the guilty get away. Never forget that this orphanage is the mother who cared for you ever since you were gifted to her and that you must returned to help her and others she will take into her fold. I know I am repeating this though I have told you many times. I pray that you will prosper and help your mother who had never let you down.

May God be with you.

- Sister Veronica

Dear Boy,

You have been such a support to me all these years. I am sorry that we could not find your family or background, though we tried hard. I know you could not make friends here, perhaps you were resentful of the fact that you had been abandoned. Boy, we can never understand God's ways as to why the innocents are punished while the guilty get away. Never forget that this orphanage is the mother who cared for you ever since you were gifted to her, and that you must return to help her and others she will take into her fold. I know I am repeating this, though I have told you many times. I pray that you will prosper and help your mother, who has never let you down.

May God be with you.

Sister Veronica.

Sr. Mary wiped away her tears and picked up Christopher's unopened letter, which had been delivered just two days earlier. She asked the boys if she should read it out to them. They said yes in chorus.

Ma,

You have been the only mother I have ever known, and I will never let you down. I feel I must do something soon to keep my promise to you. I have joined a company that sends me abroad as a courier frequently. I must take a small packet to the address provided and have a couple of days to relax and buy some goods that our company needs. Then I must collect a small packet from another address before I return. The job is easy, and I think it's an honest job. They pay me well, but I am having my doubts now. I will provide all that I earn for my mother and her children.

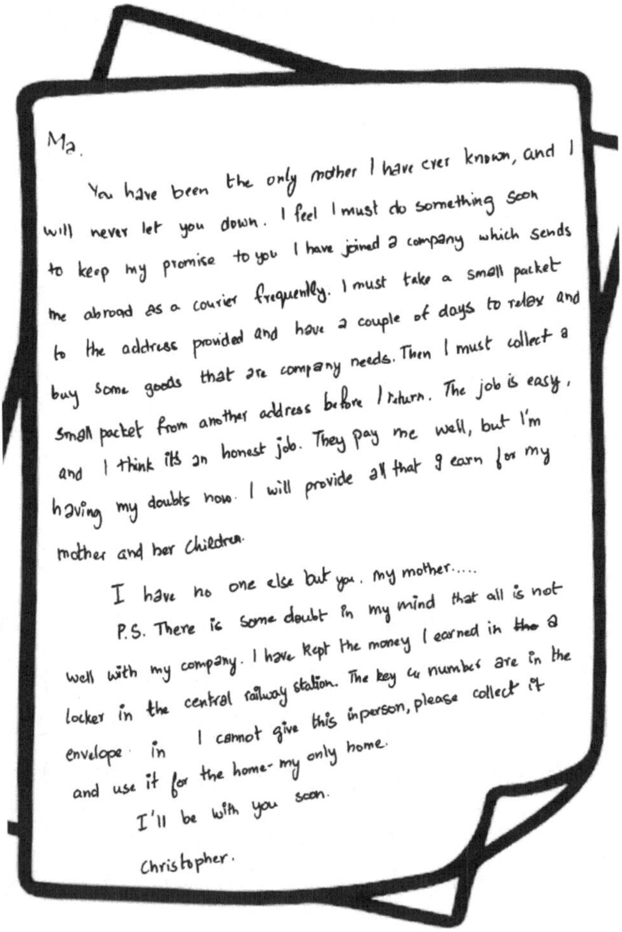

Ma,

You have been the only mother I have ever known, and I
will never let you down. I feel I must do something soon
to keep my promise to you I have joined a company which sends
me abroad as a courier frequently. I must take a small packet
to the address provided and have a couple of days to relax and
buy some goods that are company needs. Then I must collect a
small packet from another address before I return. The job is easy,
and I think its an honest job. They pay me well, but I'm
having my doubts now. I will provide all that I earn for my
mother and her children.

I have no one else but you. my mother.....

P.S. There is some doubt in my mind that all is not
well with my company. I have kept the money I earned in ~~the~~ a
locker in the central railway station. The key & number are in the
envelope in I cannot give this inperson, please collect it
and use it for the home- my only home.

I'll be with you soon.

Christopher.

I have no one else but you, my mother......

P.S. There is some doubt in my mind that all is not well with my company. I have kept the money I earned in a locker in the Central Railway station. The key and number are in the envelope. In case I cannot give this in person, please collect it and use it for the home-my only home.

I'll be with you soon.

Christopher

Sr. Mary did not attempt to hide her sorrow. The boys were wondering what the other key, which Raj had picked up, could be. Raj decided then to hand over the key to SI Mani. Sr. Mary felt that the letters and key should also be handed over to the police. Shri then collected the packet from her, placed the key chain also in it, and thanked her before leaving. Danny was then disturbed from his comfortable nap. He pulled himself from under the sofa, gave himself a good stretch and a long sigh as he left with Raj.

CHAPTER 8

THE CHASE

Raj and Shri were eager to get home early. They ran out of the Children's Home towards their house. Suddenly, a white Omni van started up and started driving towards them. Shri noticed it and shouted to Raj, "Hey, I noticed this same van was parked near the tea stall when we were talking to the SI. These chaps must be connected to the murder, let's run fast," so saying the boys sped up. But the van came very fast, and three men jumped out and began chasing them. Two were able to catch Raj, but Shri, being a fast sprinter, with assistance from Danny's barking and jumping on the third man, was able to get away. The two men pushed Raj into the van and shouted for the third fellow to jump in. The Omni sped away with Raj as a prisoner. He shouted to Shri to get help. Shri was able to note the van's number while running home fast with Danny.

Who were these men who suddenly descended on the trio? Why did they want to capture the boys, and what was their connection to Christopher?

Raj was bundled into the van, and while they were trying to tie his hands and legs, he managed to spit on them and scratch them. He had read earlier that spit would lead to culprits if DNA tests were done, and so also scratching, which would leave skin and blood under the nails. However, he was silenced with a plaster on his mouth. He struggled a lot and was able to give them a couple of hard kicks. He had wanted an adventure during the holidays, but not like this, not as a prisoner. They hit him on his head, and he acted as though he had fainted and lay still, listening to their excited banter. Evidently, the boss was scolding the guy who had hit Raj on his head, as he did not want any further accidents. "You already have a murder on your hands, don't get us into further trouble. All we wanted was to grab Christopher's loot and vanish, but you went too hard on him." So said the boss, who was addressed as Jacob.

CHAPTER 9

JACOB

Jacob had also been an inmate of the Home. He was four years older than Christopher and had been left there by his father, when his mother died. His father was very poor and could not take care of Jacob. His father planned to leave for Mumbai as he had heard that he might have better employment in that vast Industrial city. After he left, nothing more was heard of him, and Jacob remained in the Home till he had to leave at age 18, like all others.

What was the relationship like between Jacob and Christopher? Having arrived earlier, Jacob took charge of Christopher and treated him like a younger brother. He was fond of him, and Sr. Veronica encouraged Jacob to care for the younger boy who feared his surroundings and everybody. But as Christopher had no trust in any individual, he took a long time to accept even Sr. Veronica. Jacob felt he was rejected by this skinny, ugly child, and being a child himself, he could not understand this rejection. Sr. Veronica had been his favourite, and he felt he was losing her to this new entrant. She was spending more time and interest in Christopher as he needed to recuperate, and this took a long time of constant care.

Once, for Christmas, the Home had received many toys and clothes from the community members. The Sisters chose the toys and clothes suitable for each child in the Home. Jacob did not like what was given to him and wanted the battery-driven car that was given to Christopher. There was a bit of a tussle between the two, and Sr. Veronica stepped in. Jacob received a scolding and was made to return the car to Christopher. Jacob was enraged and ran away from the Home for three days. He survived in the company of a few street-smart hooligans, learning their cheating methods, but as they were bigger bullies than he was, he returned to the Home and apologised to Sr. Veronica. He realized that this place was his home. He was the senior here, the “Big Boss”, and he wanted to maintain his position.

Slowly, Jacob developed a negative attitude towards Christopher and even bullied him whenever he got a chance. However, with the kind and loving upbringing that he received from the nuns, Christopher grew up to be a kind and loving person himself. He did not hate Jacob, but he was slightly wary of him.

Jacob was aware that Christopher was the innocent courier of the company. He had worked with them himself. He had been a courier too, so he knew their modus operandi. Jacob had never forgotten his jealousy towards Christopher. As Christopher was sharing his accommodation with Jacob, the latter was able to learn of his movements. Jacob planned his move carefully, timing it with Christopher's return flight from Singapore. He called two of his old street companions and went to catch him before he went to his company. He was not aware that Christopher had gone to the Central Station directly from the airport to transfer the packet to the locker and was then on his way to the company.

Jacob and his companions <u>accosted</u> Christopher before he could reach his company and took him to their hideout, a garage. He refused to give them any information, so they beat him up till he lost consciousness. He had lost a lot of blood and appeared lifeless. Jacob realised that Christopher was dead. He panicked, and they carried the body in a gunny bag to the unused compound they had noticed when they frequented the tea shop in that locality.

Coming back to the present, Raj was blindfolded and taken to the small garage, far from other buildings. The men tied him up to a chair and started questioning him about what he knew. Raj feigned ignorance and acted dumb. The vicious guy tried to hit him again, but was stopped by Jacob. Raj gathered that these three men were not connected to the company. They were only going to rob Christopher, and Christopher must have refused to disclose any information. Raj understood from their talk that Christopher was evidently hit repeatedly, and unfortunately, the blows were fatal, leaving him dead. He had not revealed anything, despite this torture, so they brought the body to the unused compound and waited to see if anything would be revealed to them. Pressurising a little more, they threatened Raj, but he said he knew nothing more than the fact that the body was that of Christopher and that he had been an inmate of the Home. He was going home to the new Tuition Master when they caught him. He demanded to be set free.

CHAPTER 10

THE RETURN

Jacob was not sure of what he had to do with this squirming brat. He was aware that he could squeal on them and reveal their hideout. He was blindfolded again, driven to another place, and thrown onto the road while they sped away. Raj freed himself as they had not tied up his hands. He pulled off the blindfold and slowly, looked around. "Where was he?", he had no idea, as it seemed to be on the outskirts of Chennai. Hardly anybody was to be seen. He had to wait for some time, which seemed like an eternity. Finally, he was helped by a passerby, who gave him the details of this location. Thanking him, Raj walked towards the Main Road where he was able to get an auto to reach home.

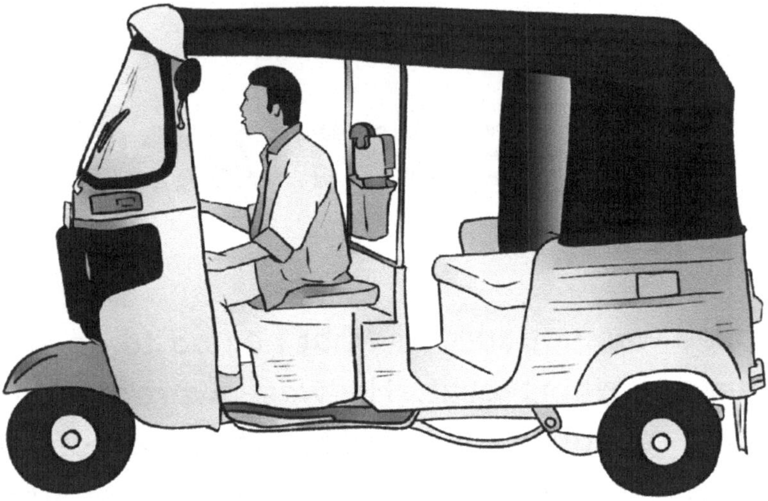

His mother, Sumana, was at home, praying to all the Gods to keep her son safe. She ran to him and hugged him tight till he wriggled out of her embrace and asked for money for the auto. The auto was paid, with a lot of haggling by Sumana, and Raj had to make her accept that he had come from a long distance and that the fare the driver was demanding was over Rs 500. She paid grudgingly.

She then turned to Raj angrily. All the fear and love had disappeared! In a shrill voice, she shouted, "Ennada, what did you think!? You thought you and Shri are great Sherlock

Holmes? Remember, you are just 14 years old and still in school." A mother's love is, at first, anxiety and fear for the safety of her son; followed by anger when he is safe and sound! This is the truth with all mothers in the universe!!

After a thorough scolding, she lovingly sent her son to have a bath, checked him for any injuries he might have sustained, and made him a few hot dosas as he was very hungry. She allowed him to call his father to inform him that he had returned safely.

CHAPTER 11

THE EVIDENCE

Meanwhile, have we forgotten Shri and Danny? They had reached home gasping, and Shri had informed his parents that Raj had been abducted. He was able to give the Omni Registration number to Sumesh, who had informed SI Mani immediately.

Simultaneously, Mani was able to locate the company where Christopher had been employed. He questioned the two men in the company, regarding Christopher, without revealing that he had been murdered. They were not aware of any developments and pleaded innocence about smuggling. They said they had sent Christopher on business matters to Singapore. "Fine then, as we found Christopher, and he would not tell us how he had some smuggled goods with him, we'll have to keep him in custody", so saying, Mani left the company.

SI Mani collected all the information from Raj when he returned. When he acted like he had fainted, he had eavesdropped on their arguments. He was able to remember the names of the three men and had heard that they only wanted to rob Christopher but had accidentally killed him. Since the loot was smuggled, Jacob had felt that the company would not call the police. Therefore, they were careless and casual about their involvement and in dealing with Raj. Raj had a faint idea of their hideout as he kept track of the distance he had travelled before they threw him out, and the kind-hearted man had given him the location from where he took the auto. SI Mani was able to locate and arrest the three criminals.

CHAPTER 12

THE LOCKERS

Mani called Sumesh to come to the Central Railway Station to open the lockers mentioned by Christopher. Sumesh, Venkat, Raj, and Shri went to the station with the packet from the Children's Home.

The station was very crowded, as it always is, and the noise was incredible. Travellers were spread out all over the place with children and luggage. Some were sleeping with their bags as pillows, and some had spread out their sheets and were having family meals. Dodging these impediments, SI Mani and the group went upstairs where the lockers were located.

Lockers No.12 and 13 were next to each other. No. 12 was opened with the key enclosed in Christopher's letter to Sister Veronica. This locker had 2 lakhs in cash. The other locker, No. 13, was opened with the key Raj had taken out of the keychain. This had the <u>hoard</u> of cash in international currencies and gold, which the smugglers were expecting.

A copy of the letter that Christopher had written to Sister Veronica was also in locker No. 12, with an added note. "I can never return fully to my mother, what she gave me. God promise mother [though you would not like me to use that phrase], this is my hard-earned money, honestly earned, though it is from a smuggler's company. I do hope you will accept it". In the other locker was a note in which he had written. "The company does not deserve this smuggled amount. As the company was cheating the government, please hand it over to our Chief Minister". What a simple, honest, and innocent soul was Christopher, despite his hard background.

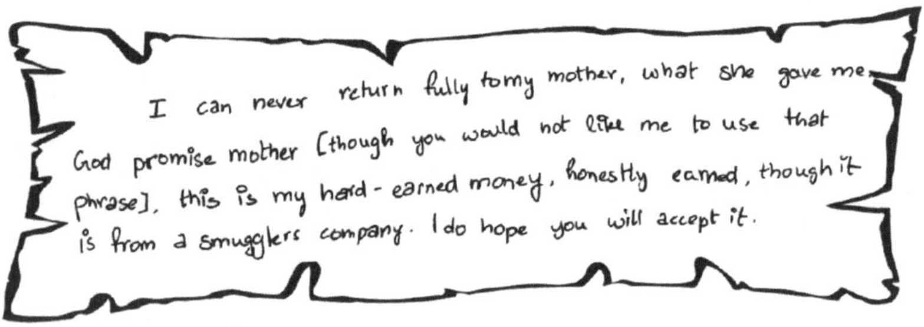
I can never return fully tomy mother, what she gave me
God promise mother [though you would not like me to use that
phrase], this is my hard-earned money, honestly earned, though it
is from a smugglers company. I do hope you will accept it.

SI Mani was happy with the outcome of this case, which was solved with the help of these intelligent and courageous boys, and more so within the same day. He praised Raj and Shri for their honesty, not forgetting Danny, for whom he presented a packet of canine treats. He congratulated Sumesh and Venkat for having given a good upbringing to their sons.

SI Mani had the last word, "Enjoy your holidays, boys, but stay clear of anymore dead bodies!"

CHAPTER 13

THE NEW TUITION MASTER

The boys went home happy and proud of themselves, forgetting about the new tuition master fixed by their parents.

The young and smart master introduced herself, "Hello, I'm Vanaja Murthy. Glad to see you. Happy to meet you both and your brown canine friend." Greeting them, this pretty, young lady bent down to pet Danny, who was happy to sniff the nice smell emanating from this person who was not shooing him away like those sweaty fellows!

The smart young lady seemed very friendly. She was dressed in a crisp, cotton sari and looked pretty and neat. Raj thought she looked like Nayanthara, his favourite actress, but Shri was thinking she looked like Vidya Balan in the movie Parineeta. Both boys were speechless.

"Hey, young chaps. Your mother was telling me that the three of you helped to solve a murder in just one day. How is that possible if you can't even open your mouths to wish me and introduce yourselves? Even this little pup is more friendly", she said, petting Danny, who was shamelessly nuzzling up to her.

Raj and Shri got out of their happy dream world and muttered "Sorry". Raj introduced himself, and Shri introduced himself and Danny. They spoke in one voice," Welcome Ma'am, very happy to meet you."

Vanaja introduced herself again and gave a brief resume of her academic background. She asked them about their strong areas and their bugbears. She had a small quiz prepared for them on various topics and current world issues as an icebreaker. "Are you ready, and would you be happy with this quiz for our first day?"

The boys chorused, "Of course, we would love it". Both were very strong in General Knowledge and Current Affairs. They were up to date with the daily news, local and global, unlike most children of their age.

That was how Vanaja earned her happy place with Raj and Shri as their last tuition master. She also made them forget Nayanthara and Vidya Balan and immerse themselves happily into Algebra, Geometry, and Arithmetics, all the math subjects.

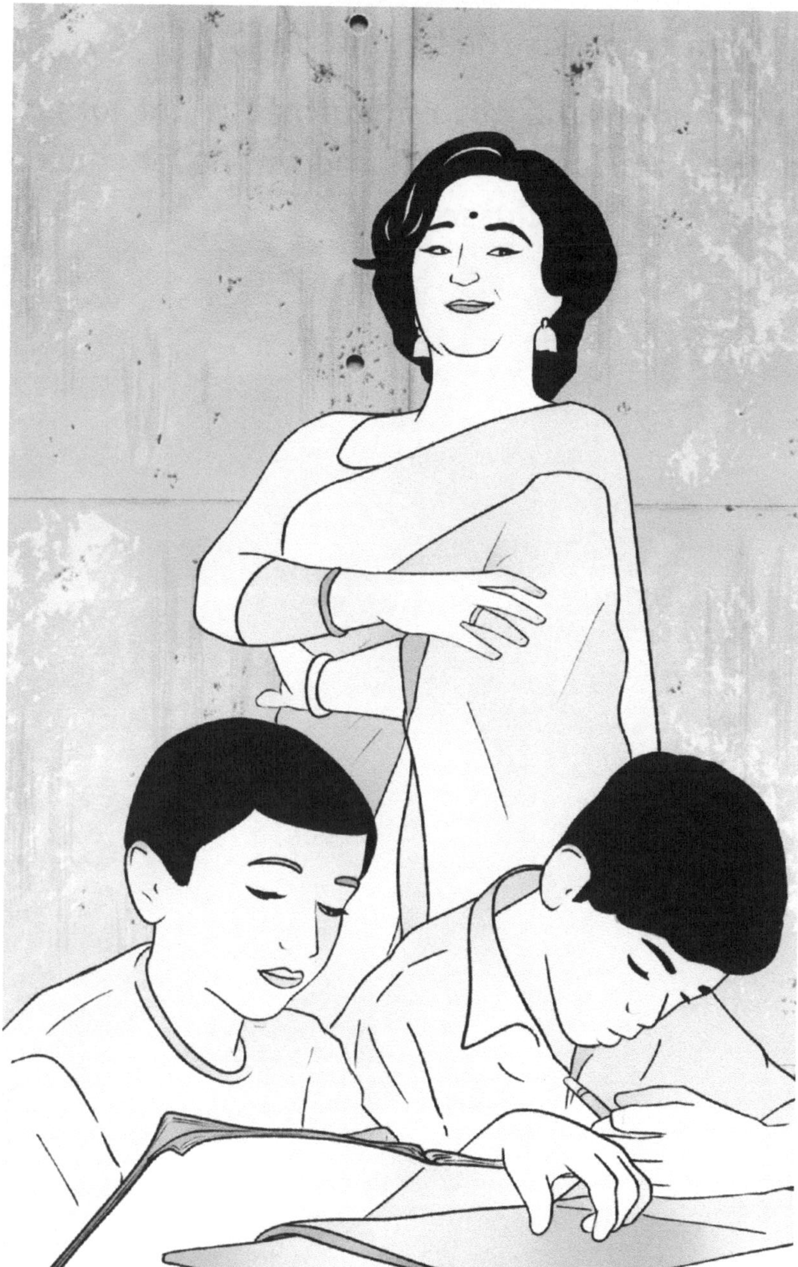

But who was the happiest?

Danny. Who got no maths but got lots of petting and lots of treats and was never chased away from the classroom!!

EPILOGUE

Needless to say, the Chief Minister donated the total amount received from the police to the Children's Home. (Was that like a second gift from Christopher? Did he return once again?)

Raj and Shri were felicitated by the Chief Minister. They received the Bravery Award given annually by the Government of India, from the President, in New Delhi. This award is given to children below 15 years for exceptional courageous deeds.

Raj and Shri got full marks for Maths in their 10th exam. This was another award they earned, shared by the surprising tuition master, Vanaja Murthy!!

Will Raj, Shri, and Danny have any more adventures in the future? We will have to wait and see!!

GLOSSARY

A to Z

Accosted – to approach or to stop

Ancillary supporting the main work

Bugbears – difficult subjects, cause of obsessive fears, anxiety and irritation

Congenial – pleasant

Dosas - (savoury pancakes made of fermented rice and lentil batter)

Eavesdropped – to listen secretly

Emanating --- the scent of a perfume or fragrance spreading closely

Enigma – mystery or mysterious

Exuberant -- full of energy and excitement

Feigned - acted

Forensic -- scientific tests used to find out about a crime or death

Hoard – to store (often secretively) money, food etc.Introspection -- thinking deeply and inwardly

Land-line -- wired, telephone connection at home

Mellifluous -- sweet, soothing, and pleasant sound as in music

Modus operandi -- a particular way or method of working

Recoup/Recuperate -- get back or get better

Rigor Mortis -- stiffening of the body after death

Shackled -- chained

Simultaneously – occurring at the same time

Squirmed – wriggle or twist the body

Tuition Master – either lady or gent, teacher

Untoward -- unexpected and unpleasant

Upbringing – raising a child, on how to behave

Upma - (a very frequent item made for breakfast in South Indian homes)

Vicious – cruel, causing hurt

WHY DID I VENTURE INTO WRITING THIS BOOK?

This is my first attempt at writing fiction. I had always written articles based on my own or others' experiences. This experiment began in the summer of 2010, when I signed up for a Script Writing Short Course under the guidance of Mr. John Edathattil, a successful script writer for movies. On the first day of the course, I told him that I cannot write fiction. He said, "Why not? All of us have a story in us. Think hard, and you will find your inspiration".

I thought hard and remembered seeing a dead body under a tree on the pavement, in a busy road in Mumbai. Nobody seemed to be bothered about it, and I wondered who this person had been and what his story could be. Further, I was always interested in dogs and children as I grew up with four elder brothers; quite a few male cousins, two sons, two grandsons, a tom-boy granddaughter, and many pet dogs. Hence, this story came to my mind, and I am happy to have completed it in just fifteen years, from 2010 to 2025!

I had also signed up for Sweta Samota's Publishing course under her banner of India Authors Academy, and learnt that publishing could be learnt easily. I had self-published two books related to my family, and they were meant for my family members only, not for sale. Now, at age 85, I have ventured into murder mysteries for young adults and children!

Good luck to my readers!!

Malathi Mohan,
Bangalore, 2025.

ACKNOWLEDGEMENTS

Where should I start when I have many thanks to convey to all my well-wishers and helpers?

I am blessed with a very large family, each with a very large heart. While I say thanks to each one of them, my very special thanks go to my granddaughter, Prerna Mohan. She helped me with making my new laptop ready to use, she designed the front and back covers of this book, and she helped with editing. All these were done with love, teaching, guiding, and even a few scoldings out of exasperation for this 85-year-old grandma, who is only up to 3rd Std. in computer usage!

I have great respect and gratitude for Sri. John Edathattil, of the Script Writing course I attended. He has appraised my story and has given a review. I had to locate him after 15 years, and he still remembered!

I thank Smt. Bharathi Babu Doraiswamy, Principal, Sri Vidya Mandir Educational

Institutions, Bengaluru, for her review and appreciation.

I am indebted to the guidance I have received from Sweta Samota, India Authors Association, Publishing Course.

I would like to thank Ms. Nihaarika Lunia for her excellent cover design and illustration

I thank my immediate family in Bangalore, my sons, Madhav Mohan and Shyam Mohan, and Shyam's family- Shalini, Nischal, and Prerna, for accommodating me and encouraging me at every stage.

I must say a special thanks to my nephew, Naresh, Nemali, for suddenly arriving from the USA and presenting me with a new laptop for my fiction writing.

A SUMMARY BY JOHN EDATHATTIL

Two Boys, a Dog, and a Murder is a charming and spirited children's novella that combines suspense, humour, and heart in a way that feels both exciting and comforting. The narrative has a warm, conversational tone, at times pausing to address universal feelings with gentle humour. "A mother's love is, at first, anxiety and fear for the safety of her son, followed by anger when he is safe and sound! This is the truth with all mothers in the universe!" Such asides make the story feel friendly and accessible, as if a kindly elder is recounting an adventure.

The theme of hope and fear is deftly balanced when Raj, Shri, and their loyal dog, Danny, discover a body near their apartment. Fear is immediate but never overwhelming. Their instinct to involve adults, to stay truthful, and to be brave without being reckless, creates a hopeful current throughout the mystery. Moments of tension (like Raj's brief kidnapping) are resolved with reassurance and warmth, reinforcing that courage and goodness prevail.

What makes the story resonate deeply is its grounding in real life. These boys aren't superheroes; they are smart, curious kids with a lovable dog and concerned parents. Their dreaded math tuition feels relatable and true to life. Their heroism is not in fighting villains but in making honest choices and sticking together through adversity.

The characters' world is vividly tangible, from the scent of the morning cocoa to Danny's barks at suspicious strangers. Danny adds joy and comic relief—"a constant companion and an accomplice in all their adventures, was Danny, the happiest of the three." His loyalty and presence make the mystery both heartwarming and light.

Finally, the moral journey the boys undertake – moving from playful curiosity to responsible action is a satisfying catharsis. They grow, not by solving everything themselves, but by learning when to act and whom to trust. The closing scenes, where the boys are honoured and the orphanage is saved, offer a moving and memorable conclusion. As Inspector Mani says with a smile, "Enjoy your holidays, boys, but stay clear of anymore dead bodies!"

REVIEWS

SAB John Edathattil

Screen Writer and Story Coach

"Written with the spirited imagination of a true, lifelong learner, Two Boys, a Dog, and a Murder is a delightful mystery where courage, curiosity, and friendship shine. Malathi Mohan- an esteemed student of mine, way back in the summer of 2010, crafted this heartwarming tale over fifteen years, with the same perseverance her young heroes embody. A charming read for children and the young at heart."

Bharathi Babu Doraiswamy

Principal, Vidya Mandir Educational Institutions, Bengaluru

The story is short and crisp. It took me back to Enid Blyton days. I thoroughly enjoyed reading it. It is a simple mystery. The theme gives scope for a lot of imagination. Wonderful venture by Malathi Mohan. Best wishes to publish many more such easy-to-read and enjoyable stories.